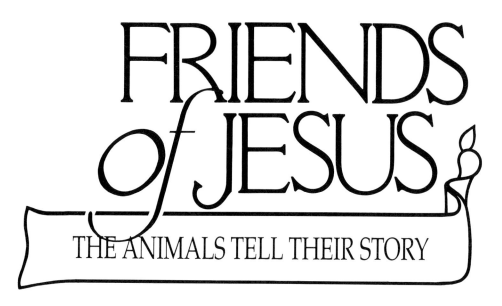

FRIENDS of JESUS

THE ANIMALS TELL THEIR STORY

Nancy Matthews

Illustrated by Maggie Downer

OLIVER-NELSON PUBLISHERS

Nashville

Published in Nashville, Tennessee, by Oliver-Nelson, Inc.,
and distributed in Canada by Lawson Falle, Ltd., Cambridge,
Ontario.

Scripture quotations are from the New King James Version
of the Bible. Copyright © 1979, 1980, 1982, Thomas Nelson, Inc.,
Publishers.

Manufactured in Singapore.

1 2 3 4 5 6 7 – 96 95 94 93 92 91

Library of Congress Cataloging-in-Publication Data

Matthews, Nancy
    Friends of Jesus / Nancy Matthews.
        , p. cm.   ,
        Summary: Relates a number of events in the life of Christ from
    the viewpoint of animals who were present.
        ISBN 0-8407-9609-9
        1. Jesus Christ—Juvenile fiction. [1. Jesus Christ—Fiction.
    2. Animals—Fiction.] I. Title.
    PZ7.M4343Fr 1991
    [E]—dc20   91-12833
                                                              CIP
                                                              AC

— CONTENTS —

—THE DOG IN THE INN—

THE DOG lived at the inn in Bethlehem. Her master was kind, but he never realized that a stone floor was an uncomfortable place for a dog to sleep. It made her old bones ache.

At night she would sneak out to the stables and jump into a spare manger. Chopped straw made a soft bed, and she would sleep soundly.

One evening, the inn was particularly busy. In the crowd were a young man and a woman who seemed very tired. They were pleading with the dog's master for a room in the inn, but he shook his head.

The couple was turning sadly away when the master had an idea. He took a lantern and led the couple away to the stables. The dog saw the master approaching and hid quietly in the manger. Shooing away the ox and ass, the master pointed to a heap of straw.

"I'll leave you the lantern," the man said. "Call me if you need anything."

In the early hours of the morning, as moonlight trickled under the stable door, the dog awoke to the cry of a baby. Looking out over the side of the manger, the dog saw the man holding a newborn baby.

The dog jumped from the manger and ran toward the couple, back and forth . . . back and forth . . . until they understood that the dog was offering the manger as a crib. The manger was soft and warm and free from drafts – the very place the dog would have chosen to lay puppies.

"Thank you," said the man to the dog as he laid the baby down. Then the dog stretched out on the floor. The hardness of the stone didn't seem to matter anymore, and she kept guard faithfully throughout the night over the couple and their child.

—THE CAMEL CARRIES—

THE CAMEL trudged through the sand carrying a king person on his back. The camel's feet ached and he was sad because he had heard people say that camels are ugly, but he held his head high and pretended to ignore his critics.

At a crossroads, two other camels joined him, and each proudly carried a king. As they galumphed along through the desert, the camel listened to the kings talking about a star. They all paused to stare at the sky and then changed direction to follow where the star led. They passed shepherds watching their flocks, and finally they reached the little town of Bethlehem.

In Bethlehem they passed a child leading a sick lamb. The child pointed to a stable behind an inn and said, "A king in a stable! Whatever next!" The camel grunted as his master got off and went into the stable to offer his gift of gold. The other kings followed, each with a jewelled jar of incense or myrrh.

The camel peered through the stable door and saw the three kings worshiping a tiny baby in a manger. The camel groaned in sorrow because he had no gift to give to the baby.

Then the wise owl, who perched in a nearby tree, opened one bleary eye and hooted, "Camel! You have carried the king across the dry desert. No other animal could have done that!"

Watching the baby King, the camel forgot that his feet ached and that people always called him ugly. The camel was content because he knew the owl was right.

—THE DONKEY TROTS—

THE DONKEY had spent most of his life searching for food among tufts of dried grass. Sometimes there was only sand where the roots had once been. Occasionally, if no one was looking, he would venture to the edge of the cornfield and steal ripe, crunchy ears.

One morning the donkey was awoken by a great commotion. Men were scurrying here and there, women were crying out and clutching their babies, and children screamed shrilly. The donkey was with his mother. He heard their master exclaim, "This mare's too old! We'd better take the colt"—and a halter was fastened round the donkey's neck and he was dragged away to the road.

The donkey overheard the words "Herod" and "Egypt" but they meant nothing to him. He stood very still while his master helped a mother, called Mary, onto his back and gave her a little child to hold. The donkey had never borne a burden before.

But now the donkey set off as fast as his little feet could trot until his master could barely keep up. They overtook many donkeys, and people trudging in the blistering sun. The little donkey knew he must hurry. He needed no bait to bribe him and no goad to drive him, because he just knew that he must reach a place of safety for the precious family quickly.

And, thanks to the donkey, they arrived in a new land, exhausted but safe.

—THE OWL LISTENS—

THE OWL perched on a rafter in the Temple one morning. He had just eaten many mice that had come out of their hiding places into the dark.

During daylight, when he was not sleeping, the owl enjoyed listening to the wise sayings of the doctors and preachers. Spell-bound, he would perch above a group of bystanders, intent on hearing everything.

It was the time of the Feast of the Passover, and this morning a family appeared in the Temple. The man, Joseph, walked ahead, while Mary followed quietly behind him.

Neither noticed that their son lingered, anxious to hear the words uttered by the wise men. The boy asked questions of the doctors that the owl had so often wanted to ask. The owl listened intently to the wise men's answers and then, hooting with satisfaction, stored them away in his memory.

The boy did not seem worried that his father and mother had moved off without him. He had more important things to think about, but the owl could tell that the boy would grow up to be the wisest man the world had ever known.

—THE DOVE ESCAPES—

THE DOVE had snowy white feathers, and she lived with her brood on a farm that grew corn. During droughts she would search for insects in the olive trees and among the parched grass nearby.

The dove was the farmer's most prized possession, but, when the time came to bring gifts to God, he knew he must give God his best gift. With tears on his cheeks, he caught the dove, put her in a small cage, and they set off on a bumpy ride on the back of an ass.

When they reached the Temple, all was chaos. Traders haggled, children scuttled hither and thither, chickens screeched, lambs bleated in terror, and a young calf mooed for his mother.

The dove was scared. But suddenly someone appeared and lashed at the traders until they fled from the holy place. In the commotion, a bar on the dove's cage broke off, and she was free to soar high in the air.

—The Goat and his Master—

Didymus the Goat was a silly goat who was always getting in trouble, eating rubbish which gave him tummy-aches, chasing venomous snakes, and wandering off into the wilderness where wild beasts lurked.

Didymus was covered with sores which itched and itched, and he kept scratching them with his little pointed hooves until they refused to heal. The herdsman, a young lad called Samuel, tried to persuade his mother to put some of her healing cream on the goat, but she refused. One night while his parents slept, Samuel opened the box of cream and spread ointment over the goat's sores himself. Then he watched anxiously, but the sores did not heal.

Samuel had heard of a man who was a great healer. Samuel sank on his knees, clasped his hands, and prayed, believing that God would help Didymus.

Suddenly there was a commotion outside. People were gathering round a man who was preaching good news. Young Samuel, leading Didymus, battled his way through the crowd and pleaded, "Oh, sir! Please, sir, heal my goat. I know you can."

An Elder tried to push him aside, but the preacher stopped, smiled kindly and said, "Your goat is healed. Your loving faith has made him whole."

New hair was growing where the sores had been.

"Thank you, oh thank you," whispered Samuel. He followed the preacher into the house.

His mother stood there with the cream in her hand. Lovingly, she put it on the man's head. She did not seem to notice the hole in the ointment which Samuel's fingers had made.

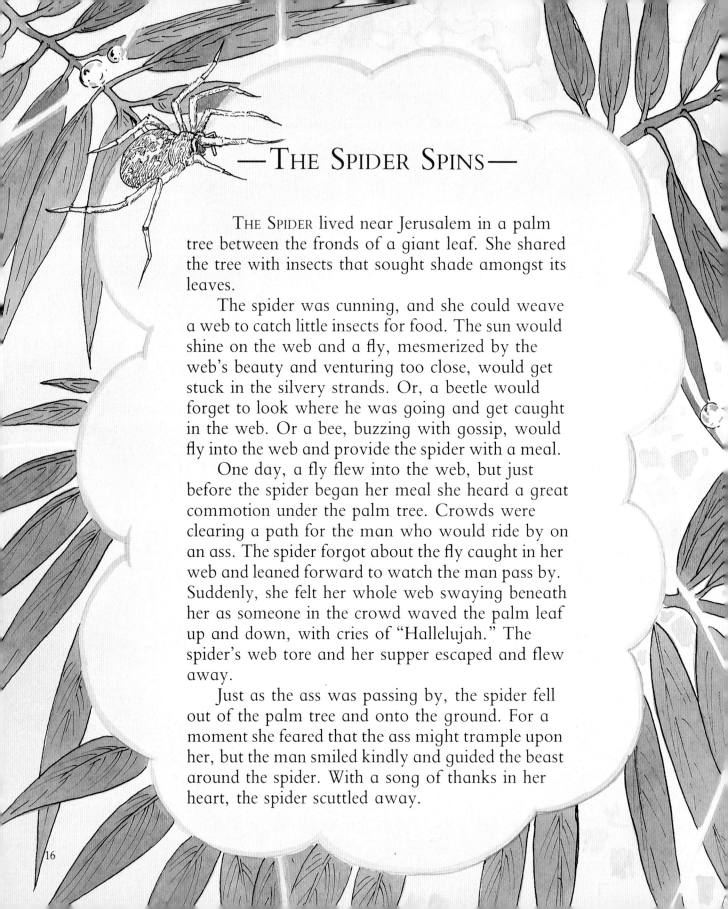

—THE SPIDER SPINS—

THE SPIDER lived near Jerusalem in a palm tree between the fronds of a giant leaf. She shared the tree with insects that sought shade amongst its leaves.

The spider was cunning, and she could weave a web to catch little insects for food. The sun would shine on the web and a fly, mesmerized by the web's beauty and venturing too close, would get stuck in the silvery strands. Or, a beetle would forget to look where he was going and get caught in the web. Or a bee, buzzing with gossip, would fly into the web and provide the spider with a meal.

One day, a fly flew into the web, but just before the spider began her meal she heard a great commotion under the palm tree. Crowds were clearing a path for the man who would ride by on an ass. The spider forgot about the fly caught in her web and leaned forward to watch the man pass by. Suddenly, she felt her whole web swaying beneath her as someone in the crowd waved the palm leaf up and down, with cries of "Hallelujah." The spider's web tore and her supper escaped and flew away.

Just as the ass was passing by, the spider fell out of the palm tree and onto the ground. For a moment she feared that the ass might trample upon her, but the man smiled kindly and guided the beast around the spider. With a song of thanks in her heart, the spider scuttled away.

—THE ROOSTER CROWS—

THE ROOSTER was proudly strutting up and down among the hens in the garden of the High Priest's palace. He had picked grain from the floor until he could pick no more, and the hens wanted to sleep because roosting-time was long past. It would soon be time for them to lay their eggs.

With a toss of his head and a gurgle in his crop, the rooster sent them off to bed. They waddled to their perches clucking contentedly while he went to the porch of the palace to see what was going on. Nearby a great crowd was gathering around a man warming himself by the log fire.

A serving maid approached the man, who shook his head. Then a priest bent low and spoke into his ear, and the man waved his arms violently.

The rooster heard a shout and the man swear loudly. Something was very wrong. The rooster felt that the man was being a coward and denying something he should have been proud to boast about. So the rooster flew up onto a beam and crowed as loudly as he could. He just *had* to shout the truth from the rafters.

The man rushed through the porch and out into the garden weeping; and then the rooster felt pity for him and fell silent.

—THE BEETLE BURROWS—

THE BEETLE was busy boring into logs in the woodshed. One day he heard a soldier ordering a cross for a man who had called himself a king. The beetle lurked in the sawdust and selected the strongest beams of wood. Then he called to all the other woodworm beetles in the woodshed. If they made enough holes, the cross could not bear the weight of the King's body.

Working frantically, they bored deeper and deeper, hour by hour through the night, digging holes and still more holes; but strive as they might they could not finish their work in time.

The Commander of the Guard ordered the man to carry the cross to the place of his own execution. Lurking in the wood, the woodworm beetle felt a heave and a lurch, and the journey began. The man climbed until he staggered. Another man took his place and continued the climb up the hill to Calvary.

The soldiers drove nails through the man's wrists and into his crossed feet and then, groaning under the strain, they raised the cross with him upon it.

The beetle's tears flowed, sad that he had not gnawed fast enough to stop the King's painful death.

"Never mind, little woodworm, you tried your best. You will be judged for your effort, not for your failure," a white dove cooed from the branch of a sycamore tree.

And then the beetle was at peace with himself.

THE BAT
IN THE CAVE

THE BAT flew into his cave at daybreak, after enjoying the cool night air.

On the previous day, while he had been hanging upside down from a ledge in the roof sleeping soundly, someone had laid a human body wrapped in burial clothes in the cave. Then the person had rolled a large rock across the entrance of the cave, making it difficult for the bat to escape, but in the cave he found a chink of light cast by the full moon and flew out into the garden.

On his return, the bat found the rock rolled aside and a heap of white clothing where the body had lain. Although he was dazzled by the morning sunlight, the bat flew into the garden at top speed to spread the good news.

First, he found two women and tried to whisper into their ears, but they only waved their arms and

drove him away. Then he told a wriggling
earthworm who, fearing that this was a trick to eat
him alive, slid his slimy body way down into the
ground.

Then he told the ass, who remembered his
journey and brayed with relief that he had trotted
fast enough.

The owl hooted that he had always known the
truth, and the camel was so pleased that he forgot
how ugly he was. The spider said how sorry she
was for all the insects she had captured in her web,
and the dove made new efforts to spread peace.
The cock could only crow with delight, the goat
rejoiced again that his sores were healed, and the
woodworm was thrilled it had ended so well.

The dog sat faithfully at his master's heels and
the whole animal world marveled.